# MAYA

## makes a

# MESS

# RUTU MODAN

# MAYA
## makes a
## MESS

A TOON BOOK BY

# RUTU MODAN

TOON BOOKS IS AN IMPRINT OF CANDLEWICK PRESS

*For Hilel,*
*who can never have too much pasta.*

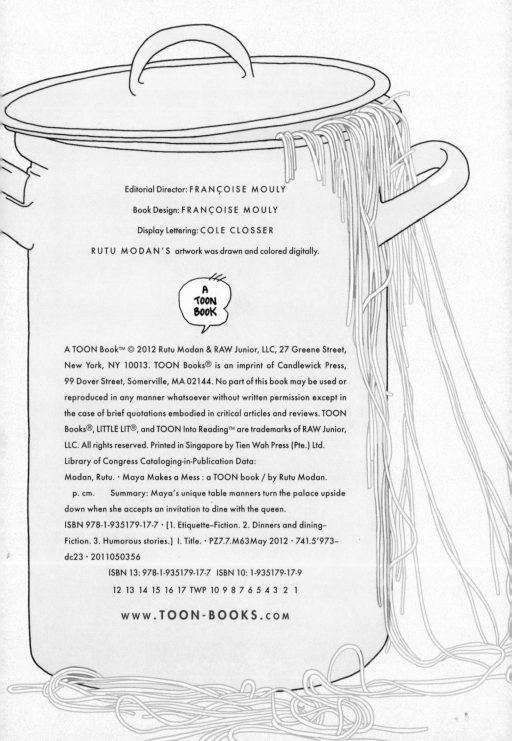

Editorial Director: FRANÇOISE MOULY

Book Design: FRANÇOISE MOULY

Display Lettering: COLE CLOSSER

RUTU MODAN'S artwork was drawn and colored digitally.

A
TOON
BOOK

Library of Congress Cataloging-in-Publication Data:
Modan, Rutu. · Maya Makes a Mess : a TOON book / by Rutu Modan.
    p. cm.     Summary: Maya's unique table manners turn the palace upside
down when she accepts an invitation to dine with the queen.
ISBN 978-1-935179-17-7 · [1. Etiquette–Fiction. 2. Dinners and dining–
Fiction. 3. Humorous stories.] I. Title. · PZ7.7.M63May 2012 · 741.5'973–
dc23 · 2011050356

        ISBN 13: 978-1-935179-17-7  ISBN 10: 1-935179-17-9

        12 13 14 15 16 17 TWP 10 9 8 7 6 5 4 3 2 1

W W W . T O O N - B O O K S . C O M

Excuse me! We are in the *middle* of dinner!

Her Majesty the Queen invites Maya to come to a dinner party. ***Tonight.***

But I *just* ate.

So what?

Juice and cookies?

Uh...

Are you all right, honey?

I've never *met* a *queen* before..

As long as you mind your *manners*, the Queen will be nice.

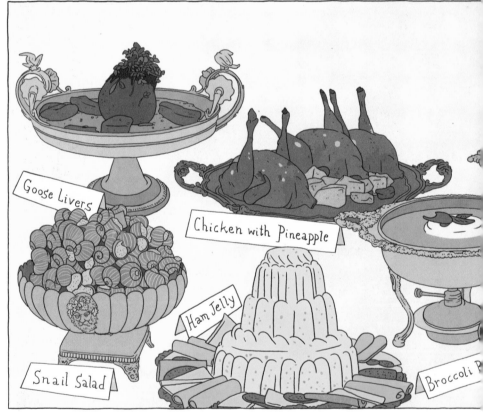

Goose Livers

Chicken with Pineapple

Ham Jelly

Snail Salad

Broccoli P

Suddenly, the room became **very** quiet.

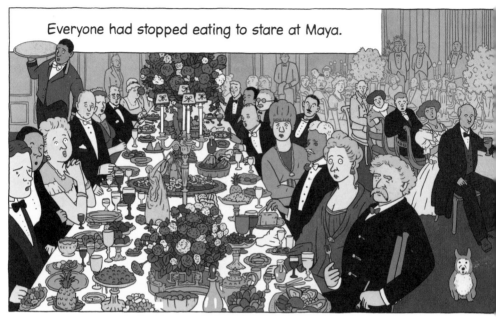

Everyone had stopped eating to stare at Maya.

**Never**–not even in the **wilds** of the kingdom–have **such** bad manners been seen.

They're going to put me in *jail*!

Didn't **anyone** teach you manners?

Well, my parents did...

Then **why**, for heaven's sake, do you **eat** that way?

It makes food taste better.

**Taste** better! Taste **better**?

**Much** better!

We shall **see**!

**Tonight**, we eat as **Maya** does.

Everyone had to listen to the Queen.

The Duke ate the chicken with his hands.
The Princess put her face in the soup bowl.
The Countess put her hands in the salad.
The Duchess fed cheese to the dog.

But the Queen outdid them all.

At last the Queen pushed away her empty plate.

Sigh!

I **say**! That **did** taste better!

From this day on, the people in my kingdom shall eat as Maya showed us.

But only on holidays!

CLAP CLAP!

How can our kingdom **ever** thank you?

Can I have dessert?

May the dessert be **served**!

Cooks came in with piles of ice cream.

The Queen asked Maya to stay forever, but she said she **really** had to get back home...

# ABOUT THE AUTHOR

RUTU MODAN'S graphic novel, *Exit Wounds*, won the Eisner Award in 2008 and has been translated into 12 languages. And even though Rutu has received many awards for illustrating other authors' books, this is the first children's book she has written as well as drawn.

This book is a collaboration: When she was a child, Rutu liked ketchup so much she used to eat it with everything, even with cookies, or straight from the bottle (but only when her parents were not around). Then when Rutu's daughter, Michal, was young, she had very bad table manners. Rutu told her: "How badly you eat! What would you do if the Queen invited you to dine at the palace?" Michal answered very seriously: "Well! It just so happens that the Queen is a VERY good friend of mine, and she told me that I eat perfectly."

# TIPS FOR PARENTS AND TEACHERS:
# HOW TO READ COMICS WITH KIDS

Kids *love* comics! They are naturally drawn to the details in the pictures, which make them want to read the words. Comics beg for repeated readings and let both emerging and reluctant readers enjoy complex stories with a rich vocabulary. But since comics have their own grammar, here are a few tips for reading them with kids:

**GUIDE YOUNG READERS:** Use your finger to show your place in the text, but keep it at the bottom of the speaking character so it doesn't hide the very important facial expressions.

**HAM IT UP!** Think of the comic book story as a play and don't hesitate to read with expression and intonation. Assign parts or get kids to supply the sound effects, a great way to reinforce phonics skills.

**LET THEM GUESS.** Comics provide lots of context for the words, so emerging readers can make informed guesses. Like jigsaw puzzles, comics ask readers to make connections, so check a young audience's understanding by asking, "What's this character thinking?" (but don't be surprised if a kid finds some of the comics' subtle details faster than you).

**TALK ABOUT THE PICTURES.** Point out how the artist paces the story with pauses (silent panels) or speeded-up action (a burst of short panels). Discuss how the size and shape of the panels carry meaning.

**ABOVE ALL, ENJOY!** There is of course never one right way to read, so go for the shared pleasure. Once children make the story happen in their imagination, they have discovered the thrill of reading, and you won't be able to stop them. At that point, just go get them more books, and more comics.

## www.TOON-BOOKS.com
### SEE OUR FREE ONLINE CARTOON MAKERS, LESSON PLANS, AND MUCH MORE.